The Man Behind The Curtain

The Man Behind The Curtain

A story by *Brandon Hughes*

Yes and So!
Oakland, CA

The Man Behind The Curtain
by Brandon Hughes

First Edition: November 2010

Copyright © 2010 by Brandon Hughes

Yes and So!
Yes and So Publishing
Oakland, CA

ISBN: 978-0-9830-6280-6
Fiction
LCCN: 2010937447

Cover design and book layout by Kristien Amer.
Cover and author photographs by Brenda Cheatham.

For my mama.

Preface

My world has changed. It is the saddest time in my life to have my mother gone; sad she's not here to see this book published, yet joyous she read it before it was. I actually believed she'd be here to see it happen. But never mind. She was genuinely happy about every little step I took in completing this book—and about any task, for that matter. There were times I felt something was missing in a scene or in certain dialogue, and I'd call her when I finally, after weeks of pondering different ideas, figured out what to do. And on the phone I sounded like a kid at a toy giveaway: completely happy. Watery eyes happy. Dance in the middle of the street with no shirt and no shoes on happy. And my mom would get happy too, just because I was. She was my cheerleader when I sat on the bench. The most gracious and encouraging person I've ever met, who just so happened to be my mother.

I was sitting at her kitchen table when she walked in after reading the manuscript for the first time. And when she walked in, she winked at me and gave me The Okay Sign. "Excellent!" she said. She was always available to listen to me read a new piece, and helped me over the phone when I ran into a choice problem. "Mama, which sounds better, this sentence or the first one? Should I take this word out? What do you think if I added this?" Even as she lay in the hospital bed throughout those many months, I'd sit in the chair or on the bed beside her and break out my manuscript. After talking with her, I'd always make my decision. Those decisions are in this book.

In her last days, my mother talked about the work we had to do before God looks at His watch and says, "Time's up." So until the clock strikes for Brandon, I promised her I'd be working through tears and a void that cannot be filled. But as long as God is God, one day will become the next, today will become yesterday, and tomorrow will become last year. Life will go on, with or without me. So I may as well do what I'm supposed to be doing while the lights are still on. I just hope my work speaks for me even after the lights go out.

My mother had always given me a reason to live. To write. To help. To give. To love. To be passionate about all of them. And so I dedicate this book entirely to her, on her birthday, for dedicating herself entirely to me, LaMont, Je'tanii, and Jasmine—my siblings. She loved us without ceasing. We love her still.

Brandon Hughes

Came to visit:
November 22, 1956

Went home:
March 22, 2010

Mama, here's the finished product.
I love you more than the word is spoken.

The Man Behind The Curtain

ONE

I thought I was being sneaky by staying up late on Saturday nights to watch TV. I learned a bunch of moves, like the snake and crane and the drunken monkey, and sometimes got out of bed and did them right in the middle of the floor while everyone else was asleep. It didn't help that my mom made me (and my annoying little brother) get up at nine the next morning for Sunday school. I hated Sunday school.

"Corey," she said, fastening that stupid top button on my collar shirt because I couldn't do it, "you're gonna stop being cranky when it's time for church. If you can get happy about baseball, you can get happy about Jesus. Now put on this clip-on tie before I clip your behin'."

I was seven, so why did I have to go to church and be in a room with my four-year-old brother and a bunch of other little kiddies and a Sunday school teacher named Mama Cece, who talked to you like a baby? And why did I have to go to school on Sunday anyway when I was just there for five days straight? I needed a break, shoooot. My daddy didn't go to church if he didn't want to. Mama Cece said that on the seventh day God rested. Well, God, me and my daddy should've been resting together.

Instead of staying up late Saturday nights, my little brother Kenny got up early Saturday mornings to watch cartoons. You should've seen him. He rushed off that top bunk like he was going to be late for work or something. Then he tried to get me out of bed to watch those silly cartoons with him. He'd pull on the blanket covering my head till I said stop. Then he'd sit Indian-style on the floor with his Smurfs cover, staring at the thirteen-inch TV screen that sat on our dresser against the wall.

Sometimes he got too excited and oohed and aahhed, laughing and talking like someone was watching TV with him. "You see dat? Dat was fresh! Dang!" *Who are you talking to, Ken?* I thought. To get him to shut up, I'd pull the cover off my head and slap my hands on top of it. Then I did what our dad did to him and sometimes me: I gave him "the look."

He'd shut up too, drop his head and look at the floor like he was sad, then lift his eyes to see if I still looked mad. I hid back under the cover to keep from laughing in his face. My brother was such a kid.

Anything he liked, I didn't like. I had to be different, and different to me was being like a grownup. So I stayed up late. That was me in 1984.

My dad worked six days a week for most of that year. On Saturday mornings he'd drop in our room while Kenny was watching cartoons, tell us he'd see us later, and remind me of my yard duties. He promised us things like renting a movie, playing a game, or buying us Rocky Road ice cream when he returned in the evening. "Oooh, yeah, Daddy," Kenny would say, rubbing his palms together. I shook my head at his childishness.

My dad would close our door. Moments later the front door shut, the car engine screeched at the startup. Off to work. My mom remained in her room, still in bed, I assumed.

I could always hear my parents on the other side of the wall in their room, laughing. Sometimes they laughed when they were supposed to be arguing. My mom especially would say random things that would throw my dad off. I wanted to be like my dad, so I listened to how he talked to my mom.

One time in the living room he was angry about my mom going on what he called "an unaffordable shopping spree." He shouted, "You can't just go around buyin' wants! The money we have is for needs! We can't afford wants!" My dad had a way with words and always made a lot of sense too.

My mom waited with her arms crossed before she said something. "Well, what about when Michael Jackson's curl caught on fire in the Pepsi commercial?"

I looked at my dad. He was biting down on his lip and looking at the window, trying hard to stay mad.

My mother continued. "What, I can't buy a Pepsi no more? Huh?" She threw her hands up and flapped them down on her thighs with a loud slap. Before my dad could say anything, her arms were wrapped around him. Her head titled back with her chin up to look in his eyes. "I'm sorry, baby, 'kay?" she said.

He stared back in her light brown eyes and ran his fingers through her ponytail that went down the middle of her back. He was shaking his head, almost smiling.

"And don't worry, baby," she said. "I bought you something too."

"Corrina, that's what I mean. I don't need—"

"Honey. Just look in the bag." She grabbed the white bag of stuff from off the couch and handed it to him. He pulled out a pair of—

"Pink panties?" he said.

"Yeah, and your bra's in there too." She snatched them. "Gimme my panties. Keep looking."

My dad pulled out a thick blue-and-white-checkered shirt that nearly took up the whole bag. He unfolded it, held it up. "A Pendleton," he said.

"Yes," she said, twirling her pink underwear with her finger, "and that's something you need, instead of those skimpy little windbreakers you wear."

"Ah, thank you, suga." He leaned over and kissed her. "Looks better than the one ol' Gregor has. You get me anything else?" He grinned.

"No," she said, and he frowned. "Well, nothing other than these two things."

"What two things?" he said, raising one eyebrow.

"These panties and that Pendleton. They're your pajamas tonight." She flicked the panties off her finger, and they landed on his face, then she took off down the hallway. Kenny and I laughed. My dad chased her around the house, laughing as she screamed. They were at it again.

TWO

Mr. Gregor was an old, quiet next-door neighbor who kept to himself. I guess he was in his late sixties. Everyday he wore either sky-blue or dark-blue jeans, a white T-shirt, and a pair of black church shoes—the loafers with the two tassels on top. If it was cold out, he wore his checkered Pendleton, the one like my dad's. Except Mr. Gregor's was black and white and worn out, not blue and white and new. He had a perfectly trimmed gray mustache and a head of short gray hair. Some ladies thought he was handsome, saying they bet he was fine when he was younger.

Mr. Gregor would sweep the already clean walkway that led up to his house, or tend to his beautiful red and white rose bushes behind the chain link fence around his yard. Once in a while I'd see him talking to my dad, but only small talk, when my dad was going or coming from work. Since Mr. Gregor didn't talk much, my dad didn't press him. I noticed he never looked my dad in the eye when he talked. He looked at everything else: the fence, the ground, the water feeding his rose bushes, or the rose bushes drinking his water.

Sometimes I got a whiff of those roses when I was near the fence. I'd close my eyes and breathe in, then wonder if I was behaving girly. Whenever my mom was upset or disappointed with me, I thought about jumping over that fence and stealing some roses to give her as an apology. But when I imagined someone like the Browns, who lived next door to us on the other side, catching me in Mr. Gregor's yard or climbing over the fence, I'd change my mind. Word would get to my dad, and I didn't want him thinking his son was a thief. Mama would have to settle for an "I'm sorry," or a letter with a big heart at the bottom.

If my friends and I weren't playing a full game of baseball at the elementary school nearby, we were at my house. We traded cards, played catch, 3 Flies Up, practiced our bunts, or played rundown, using torn-off pieces of cardboard. When the ball accidentally went into Mr. Gregor's yard while he was outside, we made O's with our mouths and grinned at each other.

"Sorry, Mr. Gregor," I always said, as he took his time getting the ball. He never said anything back, and he never threw the ball back either. He'd just put his arm over the fence and drop it from his hand.

"Thank you, Mr. Gregor," I said, and turned to my friends who were covering their mouths, laughing.

Sometimes the ball went over, and Mr. Gregor wasn't around. Since his gate was always locked, we dared each other to jump over and get it. But all it took was the "what if" chances of my dad finding out, and the daring stopped. Then sure enough, either the next or the same day, the ball would be back in our yard, barely a foot away from the fence.

When the movies *Beat Street* and *Breakin'* had come out, everybody in the 'hood wanted to break-dance. My friends and I flattened a cardboard box my dad had given us and laid it on the cement as our dance floor. My best friend Joshua brought the boom box. One day, when Mr. Gregor was outside feeding his rose bushes, I got frustrated while spinning on my back. The cardboard was wearing out, bending too much in the middle, making me spin slower.

I got up frustrated, kicked the cardboard and called it a piece of junk. I told my friends to walk with me to Emby (the grocery store on East 14th Street) to see if they had any big boxes by the Dumpster. But they only had weak little ones. When we got back to my house, Mr. Gregor was gone, but there was a big cardboard box, already flattened, leaning against the fence in my yard. In the same place where Mr. Gregor normally dropped our baseballs.

People told me I was raw at breakin', a young Boogaloo Shrimp (a.k.a. Turbo in *Breakin'*). But I'd rather have been a baseball player than a dancer. Baseball was my thing. My brother Kenny on the other hand, if he wasn't playing tag with his best friend Gary Jr., the Browns' son, he was running around the yard shooting at or talking to imaginary friends. What a kid.

Mr. Gregor paid more attention to me than he did to my brother. So since he was going to be watching, I gave him a show. I'd throw pop-ups and catch them behind my back. Or show off my Rickey Henderson snatch catches. My friends would throw me some fly balls, and just when the ball was about to land, I'd flick my glove out and catch it, then snatch my arm behind my back right after, just like Rickey.

Being next door, Mr. Gregor had a front-row ticket. He was the audience. My audience. He's the reason I have a story to tell.

THREE

Whenever my friends and I caught Mr. Gregor staring at us, he put his head down and kept sweeping. And if any man dropped by to see my dad or to throw us some pitches or fly balls, Mr. Gregor ended his sweeping duties. He basically swept his behin' right into the house.

I remember the time Boobee, my father's nephew, came to teach my friends and me how to throw a curveball. Now Boobee was cool, my favorite older cousin who taught me everything I know about baseball. He was the starting pitcher on the varsity baseball team, to me the rawest on the field.

Boobee lived only a few blocks away, so he came through all the time. He'd ride on his chrome Mongoose bike with the red tuff wheels, the red seat with the matching chain wheel and chain, the red pedals and red handlebar grips. Hecka fresh. Instead of parking his bike inside our yard, he'd lay it down right in the middle of the sidewalk. Sometimes he'd come inside the house and look out the window, daring somebody walking down the street to touch it. At fifteen, he already had a reputation in East Oakland.

One day Mr. Gregor turned to see Boobee coming around the corner, after he saw how excited my friends got when I pointed and said, "There go Boobee." Mr. Gregor looked at Boobee and then at the ground, at Boobee, then at the ground. Boobee just stared at him while cruising on his bike. By the time Boobee's handlebars hit the ground, Mr. Gregor was already in his house.

Sometimes while playing, we saw Mr. Gregor peeping at us behind the yellow curtain at the window on the side of his house. We just figured him to be an old man who wished he was young again. But Boobee thought different. After our curveball lesson, Boobee walked us to the liquor store on 100th and Walnut to buy us some candy. Because they always asked, one of my friends got to ride his Mongoose on the way. It didn't matter who rode it there, I just knew I'd be riding it on the way back. Anyway, Boobee asked me, while my friends were ahead of us: "Wassup with that ol' man playin' peek-a-boo behin' the curtain?"

"Mr. Gregor?" I said. "He ah-ight. Just old and bored. Ain't got nothin' better to do."

Boobee laughed with a twisted grin. "Yeah, potna kinda weird," he said. "But as long as he don't step out of line he cool. 'Cause if he do—if anybody do—me and my homeboys will come through and make the wrong kinda noise. And it won't be firecrackers, li'l cuz. Won't be firecrackers."

Boobee and his homeboys didn't have to worry. Mr. Gregor was just an old man with no friends. Nobody—at least I never saw anybody—came to visit him. No one got out of their car and said, "Hey, Mr. Gregor, ol' buddy ol' pal, I'm here!" and then wait for him to skip down those three steps of his, unlock his gate, shake their hand and invite them on in. Just how he avoided eye contact with people made it seem as if he didn't want friends. But I thought he really did, just didn't know how to make them. That's why he peeked from behind the curtain.

My mom often bought extra food for homeless people who hung around the Kwik Way fast-food parking lot, or who walked up to our car in the drive-thru and asked her to buy them a hamburger. And she could barely afford food for us. I thought they were homeless because they didn't have any friends. Friends would have offered them a place to stay, some food to eat. I felt sorry for them as I did for Mr. Gregor. Except Mr. Gregor wasn't hungry or homeless. He was friendless. Boobee didn't understand that.

FOUR

The rumor was that his wife had died way before we moved into the neighborhood. Something about an allergic reaction to pain medication. I overheard the "two plump women"—as Aunt Angie referred to herself and our neighbor, Mrs. Brown—gossiping about what had happened.

My aunt Angie, who was only a little fat, and Mrs. Brown, who was really fat, loved to sit in the folding chairs on Mrs. Brown's porch and talk about whoever and whatever. Whenever Aunt Angie told a story, she acted it out. She changed her voice to sound like whoever she was talking about. She did her hands this way, her eyes that way, her mouth another. The day they were talking about Mr. Gregor's dead wife, I was playing catch near the fence separating our yard from the Browns'.

Aunt Ang' didn't even live in our neighborhood, but she knew more than anyone else. She said Mr. Gregor was bitter and lonely after his wife died, that his wife was sitting at the kitchen table watching TV on that day, complaining about a minor headache.

"When the headache got real bad," Aunt Ang' said, "she called out for her husband. 'Oh, Gregor. Gregor, honey, please . . . please stop the noise. It's killing me. Seriously, sugar dumpling.'"

"Girl," Mrs. Brown giggled, "you know good and well she ain't said no 'sugar dumpling.'"

"Hush up," Aunt Ang' said. "Anyway, that is what she said—or tried to say—but ol' Gregor couldn't hear her. See, he was doin' some hammerin' in one of the bedrooms. With the door closed since he knew she had a headache and e'rythang. And when he went in the kitchen to get some mo' nails," she shook her head, "there she was. His wife of thirty-seven years. Lyin' on the floor wit' her hand over her heart, like she was doin' the Pledge of Allegiance."

I glanced over and Mrs. Brown was covering her mouth, giggling again. But Aunt Ang' stayed serious, staring out into the street. Mrs. Brown noticed and cleared her throat, stopped giggling.

"Her last words to Mr. Gregor came in a whisper. 'Why couldn't . . .'"—Aunt Ang' whispered—"'you just . . . wait till . . . tomorrow?'"

Aunt Angie took a long puff of her cigarette and stared sadly at the ground like the wife was a friend of hers. I stopped throwing the ball. She stood up, walked to the iron rail in front of her. She leaned her head back and looked at the sky, blew smoke out toward it.

"Yeah," she said, "ol' Gregor called her name over and over as he held her, thinkin' he heard her cryin' out to him while he was hammerin', but thought it was just his imagination. Well," she turned and looked at Mrs. Brown, "he never forgave himself for it."

"Umph, umph, umph," Mrs. Brown said, shaking her head. "That's so sad. Common sense woulda told the man not to be hammerin' any damn way if his wife got a headache. I don't care if the room door was shut wit' a hundid deadbolts on it—you can hear a man hammerin' in his house if you outside on the street. Po' thang. What was his wife's name again?"

"Ah . . . I think her name was Advil."

"Girl, cut it out," Mrs. Brown said, laughing. "You know good and well that po' thang's name whatn't no Advil."

"Chil', I can't remember what her name was— hell, I don't even know if that's how the story happened."

Mrs. Brown looked at Aunt Angie like she was

crazy. Then they both cracked up laughing. I smiled and shook my head, played catch again.

"How I'm gonna know the whole story if the man don't even talk to nobody?" Aunt Ang' said with her hands on her hips.

"Ang', you somethin' else."

My dad said Aunt Ang' was like the tabloids—she mixed truth with lies. "Gary, man, that woman is a gossiper," he said to Mr. Brown about his sister-in-law, "and most gossipers don't know anything but hear everything. They only have a piece, but can't wait to give you the whole." When Mr. Brown laughed and said his wife was the same way, I wanted to tell them what Aunt Ang' had said about Mr. Gregor's wife. But my dad would've told me to stay out of grown folks' business.

FIVE

My dad and Mr. Brown—or Gary, the grownups called him—were best friends. Sometimes they'd just chill out in the backyard, talking and listening to music. Other times they lifted weights. My dad was five-six, one hundred fifty-five pounds, straight cut, all muscle. And Mr. Brown . . . well, I'll just say when my friends and I watched the movie *Enter the Dragon*, they said my dad was Bruce Lee and Mr. Brown was Bolo.

With biceps bigger than my brother's head—and Kenny had a big head—Mr. Brown was so buff we called him the Hulk, from *The Incredible Hulk*, the TV series. He even slapped on the green paint and torn-up clothes a couple Halloweens just for us. And we'd stand outside his front gate in our costumes, calling him. "Come on out, Mr. Hulk. Hulk! Trick-or-treat, Hulk." And we'd laugh and be scared for no reason since we knew him. Until some innocent kids who didn't know him walked through his gate.

We followed behind them, grinning and giggling, careful not to tell them what we knew. And before they reached the stairs, the Hulk busted out of the house, roaring and throwing the chairs from his porch across the yard. One year we didn't get out of the yard fast enough from laughing so hard and yelling and shoving each other, and the Hulk grabbed and lifted me up over his head like he was going to throw me. I just laughed. But the other kids, who came for trick-or-treating (or just for treats), were running and screaming down the street.

Sometimes at night when my dad and Mr. Brown were out back, I'd sneak out the side door in my pajamas and squat against the side of the house, peek around the corner at them and listen. Every now and then I glanced at the side windows of Mr. Gregor's house and wondered if he was peeking at me while I was peeking at them.

My dad and Mr. Brown talked about football and, going to work and working hard but hardly getting paid and, being married and how women are and, how they should be and, how they shouldn't be and, a whole lot of other stuff. Like stuff they did when they were younger. Like the time they got arrested for fighting.

My dad said when he first got to high school a lot of girls liked him, and because of it a lot of boys didn't. A popular senior was one of those boys. He gave my dad these crazy I-wanna-kick-your-butt-because-I'm-jealous looks whenever he walked by. "I knew I'd have to put hands on this chump one day," my dad said. And the day came.

Between classes, the boy claimed my dad was looking at his girlfriend in the hallway. The boy said, "Eh! You lookin' at my girl, li'l man? Eh, punk, you hear me talkin' to you?" My dad said he ignored him, kept walking. But then the boy came from behind and pushed him. He should've stuck with the name-calling, my dad said, because when he turned around, he slapped a textbook across the boy's face so hard it knocked him on his back. Mouth bleeding, a tooth missing. My dad got suspended and the boy pressed charges.

"But," Mr. Brown asked, "did you get the girl?"

"Can Michael Jackson backslide?" my dad said. And that was that.

Mr. Brown did dumbbell curls as he told his story. He said he went to jail for whuppin' a boy in front of his house for making fun of his shoes. The soles flapped when he walked because they were no longer glued to the shoes. They were real cheap, Mr. Brown said, cheaper than Pro Wings. Anyway, the boy called him poor, said his mama better get him some new shoes because the ones he had on looked like they were talking. Mr. Brown said he ran up on the boy faster than a finger snap and started decking him in the mouth in his own front yard. And when the boy's father—who had been sitting on the porch laughing as his son talked smack—tried to jump in, he beat him up too. Mr. Brown said he left them on the ground whimpering, huddled up. Like father, like son.

When he finished his story, Mr. Brown set the dumbbells down and flexed his arms. "I wish a fool would try to step to me nowadays," he said, kissing each bicep. "I'm six-three, two-fifty. I'll rearrange his whole body structure. Give him before-and-after pictures."

I told my friends the story, and they were like: "For real? Dang, he really *is* the Hulk."

SIX

Since my dad and Mr. Brown liked lifting weights, they turned part of our backyard into an outdoor gym. The ol' school cars they promised to fix one day took up their garage, so it was either our backyard or Mr. Brown's. They had the bench press and dumbbells, barbells and curl bar, triceps bar—all that and a small radio. My favorite part of their workout was seeing them on the bench press. Watching them take turns pumping that iron made me want to have a turn too.

One Saturday when I was supposed to be doing chores and my dad was supposed to be working, he came home because he had forgotten something, and saw me through the window in his bedroom—lying on the bench press, reaching for the bar.

"Corey!" he whispered, and I jumped. The window was open just a crack so he had bent over some and cocked his head to the side, his mouth by the crack. Then he stood up straight and held up his index finger to me as if he couldn't talk right then and there. I figured because my mom was sleeping. And in his black steel-toe boots, black Levi's jeans, and his blue-and-white-checkered Pendleton, here he comes.

"Corey, what I tell you about foolin' with these weights?"

"Um . . . sorry, Daddy."

"You sorry, huh?" He walked over to the bench press and tapped the bar. "You see this here?"

"Yeah," I said. He gave me *the look*. "I mean, yes."

"This is two hundred and twenty-five pounds. If it falls on you, in seven days we'll be having your funeral. You understand?"

"Yes."

"Good. Now if you want muscles in your chest do some push-ups . . . I'll show you before I head back to work." He got on the ground. "Keep your body straight like this, arms in front of you and under you. And then . . . all the way down," he went, "all the way up," he came.

As he did a few more, I felt someone spying on us. I looked over and saw Mr. Gregor's head just before it dashed away from the window curtain in the back of his house. My dad got up. "Your turn," he said.

I got down and tried. "Like this?" I said.

"Naw, naw—you doin' it like a girl. Get your knees off the ground. Now stay like that. We'll do it together. Ready?"

"Uh-huh," I said, smiling.

He got down beside me. "All the way down," we went, "all the way up," we came. "There you go. You doing it, man. A few more."

He stood and watched me do them by myself. I thought I was fresh. I glanced over to see if Mr. Gregor was watching but couldn't tell.

"That's my little man right there. Keep it up, and ya chest'll be hard as a rock," he said, beating his chest with his fist. I got up to join him; he squatted so I could.

"Feel that?" he said. I nodded and smiled. "It all started from push-ups."

So that's what I did sometimes between chores—push-ups. I'd put the broom down and hit ten real quick, sweep a little and hit five more. I was becoming a man. Later, I'd go and stand in front of the long mirror behind the bathroom door, toss my shirt, hold my hands together in front of me, and look tough while I flexed. I was trying to get my chest to bounce up and down like my dad could do.

SEVEN

Every Saturday morning I had chores. I picked up trash in or near our yard, swept the driveway, the walkway, the sidewalk and curb in front of our house, the front and side porch, the backyard, and raked up the leaves on the side of the house too. I also watered the grass, both front and back yard.

Now when it came to helping me with chores, my dad only said that Kenny could help. The key word was "could." In my case, these chores weren't something I could do, they were something I'd better do. All Kenny had to do was try and make up his bed. It looked messy whether he tried or never bothered to. The kid couldn't help me anyway, I did a man's job. Poor fella couldn't even make his own bed.

It was chilly that morning as I did my chores. The sun wasn't out yet, only clouds. I wore my black hooded sweatshirt, the one Boobee gave me when it got too small for him. I messed around in between sweeping the sidewalk. I walked while twirling the broom to each side of my body with my hands, pretending a bad guy was coming toward me before I swung it like a bat.

Then I spun around and did it the other way. While I was busy being a tough guy, I heard a car dippin' behind me, bumpin' "It's Like That" by Run DMC. I turned around and the music died down.

"Look at eem," Boobee said, riding shotgun and hanging out the window. "That boy out here practicin'—huh, li'l cuz? I might have you teach me some moves."

Boobee's friend, an eighteen-year-old named Mighty Mike, had pulled up in his '75 Ford Granada. The only one like it in the 'hood: four-door, metallic blue with flakes, ragtop with the knuckles, show lights on the sides, woofers in the back, sitting on trues and vogues. Funky fresh! Fresher than any Tough Wheel that Kidco put out.

Two fine girls were in the backseat. One was light-skinned with a feathered hairdo, and the other was dark-skinned with a mushroom, like Tootie from *The Facts of Life*. Tootie had her little mirror out, messing with her hair as I walked to the car. All four of them looked like they just woke up.

"Wassup, li'l cuz?"

"Wassup, Boobee?" I said, and when he put his hand out we slapped each other five. "Sup, Mighty

Mike?"

"Wassup, young dude?"

"Ah, he's so cute," the light-skinned girl said.

"Girl, he is," the other one said, putting a scarf over her hair.

"Uh-oh, look at eem. They diggin' you, li'l cuz," Boobee said, smiling. Making me smile too. "Uncle Keith gotchu workin' early, blood—ain't nobody outside but you."

"I know, 'cause everybody still sleeping. How come you up so early?"

The girls laughed.

"Oh, well, see, me and Mighty 'bout to drop these girls off down the street so they can do some street cleanin' and—"

"Yo cousin is lyin'," the dark-skinned girl said, grinning.

"No I ain't, li'l cuz," Boobee said with a straight face. "We gon have 'em get on the ground and scrub the sidewalk from Walnut to Bancroft. They'll be cool though, they got knee pads in the trunk." The girls were laughing so hard they started clapping. "Then we gon have 'em turn around and come back, sweep what they scrubbed." He turned and pointed at the girls.

"And y'all better be done by noon, hear me? Matter fact, hand me that broom, li'l cuz."

I smiled, watching the girls crack up. They pushed the back of Boobee's head and told him to shut up with his short self. Mighty Mike had his head down and eyes closed, snickering.

"Eh, hold up, hold up," Boobee said, bobbing his head. "Turn the music up, Mighty. Li'l cuz, you ready?" I smiled. I already knew what he wanted me to do. "Y'all watch this," he said.

I turned around and laid the broom against the fence. My back was still to them as I slowly pulled the hood over my head, bouncing my leg to the beat. "Uh-oh," the girls said. That made me grin. I was still grinning as I turned around, breakdancing.

"Look at eem, look at eem," Boobee said, and the girls said, "Haaay, go 'head . . . go 'head . . . go 'head," while cheesing and bobbing their head. I was breakin', pop-locking and backsliding. I ended with one leg in front of me while leaning back on the other, arms folded, nodding.

"Yaaaaay," the girls said while clapping. "That was def."

"Yeah, you clean, li'l cuz," Boobee said, holding his hand out the window. And after I gave him five, the girls were still cheering for me as they put their hands out too. They had me all grinning and stuff, with their fine selves.

"You raw," Mighty Mike said, reaching over to give me five too. "Like Lee from *Beat Street.*"

"I know, huh," Boobee said. "Oh yeah, before I forget, I gotchu somethin', li'l cuz."

"For real? What?"

"You'll see. I'll bring it later, I promise. Ah-ight?"

"Ah-ight then," I said and slapped him five again, and the girls waved and said, "Bye, cutey—you was dope," and Mighty Mike said, "Ah-ight, young dude," and pulled off, bumping his music.

After sweeping the sidewalk and curb, I got started on the front yard. I used a plastic Emby bag to put pieces of trash in. I was bending down to pick up a candy wrapper between the driveway and the chain link fence that separated our yard from Mr.Gregor's, when, out of nowhere, on the other side of the fence, there he was. I first saw the tassels bounce a little on one of his shoes, between the tall grass along the fence. Looked up some and saw the jeans and the Pendleton.

Looked all the way up, and he was staring at me.

"You're a responsible young man," Mr. Gregor said. "I like that."

"Thank you," I said, noticing he was a little taller than my dad. "Just doing my chores."

"Chores, huh? Son, I'd say you're a young landscaper—and a good one too. If I didn't do my own yard, I'd hire you."

I turned away all shy and stuff, smiling. Something Kenny would do. I stopped as soon as I realized. I tucked my lips in my mouth so I wouldn't do it again, and turned and looked him straight in the eye. My dad said if you look a man in the eye, he'll respect you. So that's what I did.

He started asking grownup questions, like: "What do you think about the economy?" and "President Reagan is something else, ain't he?" I just said, "It's fine" and "Uh-huh" and "I think you're right." He chuckled like he knew I didn't know what I was talking about, which was true. But still, he didn't have to laugh. So when he asked, "What grade are you in?" I rolled my eyes and kept picking up trash.

EIGHT

Between the fence where the grass was left uncut, a piece of trash sat half on his side, half on mine. I almost tossed it in the plastic bag with the other crap till I noticed what it was—the Oakland A's rookie card of my favorite player, # 35, Rickey Henderson. My best friend Joshua had the card but never wanted to trade it, always kept it at home. So "Whose is this?" I mumbled. Mr. Gregor came over and set his arms on top of the fence, folded his hands.

"Whatcha got there?" he said.

"Somebody lost their Rickey Henderson card."

"Somebody lost it?"

"Yeah—I mean, yes. Look." I handed him the card.

He looked at it like he was making sure who it was. He turned the card over and back again. "Yeah, that's Rickey all right," he said. "A good player, ain't he?"

"He's the best," I said proudly. "Whoever lost

it is stupid. If it was mine, I woulda never lost it—and it's new too, shoooot."

"Well, it's yours now." He handed it back to me.

"I know, huh," I said, beginning to smile.

"Yeah. Finders keepers, losers weepers."

"I know, huh," I said, slipping the card into my back pocket.

"So tell me why you like Rickey so much," he said, folding his arms and smiling.

"'Cause he's the coolest and the fastest and he stole one-hundred-and-thirty bases in 1982 and . . . he's from Oakland, and um—he's just the best base-ball player in the world."

"I see," Mr. Gregor said with raised eyebrows. "You ever heard of James 'Cool Papa' Bell?"

"Cool Papa . . . hmm," I said, looking at the sky and tapping my finger against my chin, trying to remember this person I'd never heard of. "Naw, don't think so. Why? That's your friend?"

"No, no," he said, smiling. "But he was one baseball player who may've been faster than Rickey Henderson."

"Uh-uh, ain't nobody faster than Rickey, tsk.

And I ain't never heard of no Papa Cool."

"It's Cool Pa—"

"Well, Cool Papa then."

"You may not have heard of him because he played in the Negro League."

"The Negro Lea—wait, he was a Negro?"

"That's right," he said, leaning the side of his body against the fence.

"Negroes had their own baseball league because white folks wouldn't let them play in the majors."

"Oh."

"Yeah," he said, "I hear Cool Papa was so fast he could turn out the light and be in the bed before the room got dark."

It took me a second before I got what he said . . . . "Nuh-uh, ain't nobody that fast."

"I'm serious," he said with a straight face.

"No, you not."

"Yeah, man, they say he was faster than the Roadrunner."

"Nuh-uh."

"They say he ran around the bases going, 'Beep-beep.'" He made his eyes big when he said it, had me laughing. "All right, listen," he said. "I got a query for you."

"'Kay, where is it?" I said, not knowing what a query was.

He asked me who the greatest home-run hitter of all time was, and when I told him Hank Aaron, he said no, but I was close.

"You know who hit more than him?" he said.

"Um, nobody," I said in a smart-aleck way.

"Aha. But there was someone in the Negro League."

Here he goes talking about these Negroes again.

"Josh Gibson was his name," he said. "They called him the black Babe Ruth. 'Cept he was better than Babe Ruth, so they called Babe Ruth the white Josh Gibson."

I looked at him like he was crazy.

"They say he hit about eight hundred home runs in his career, one right out of Yankee Stadium. Nobody else has done that. Now Hank got his start in the Negro League, but Josh and Cool Papa remained there."

I'd never heard of those Negroes, never knew they had a league. See, I thought Negroes were only those black people from long time ago who I saw in black-and-white on TV and who got beat up by white people but kept on marching and singing with "Marther" Luther King. I didn't know I was a Negro too.

"So," I said, rubbing my chin, "you telling me this Josh Negro hit more homers than Hank Aaron?"

And he said yeah, and I said 'cause Hank Aaron hit seven-hundred fifty-five home runs—to show him I knew something too—and he smiled real proud and said he was impressed that I knew my stuff. And I said you doggone right, shooooot (but only in my mind).

"Um, Mr. Gregor," I said, squinting at him. "Did you play in the league of Negroes too?"

"Oh, nooo. I never played much of sports. I was never good at them," he said, sounding sad with a frown on his face. Then he dropped his head, stared at his tassels. I felt bad for him.

"Unlike you," he said, his eyes now on me. "I've never seen a kid who can play as good as you. Or who's as fast as you. I watch you. I think you're the next Rickey Henderson. In fact, I'ma start calling you Little Rickey."

I smiled a little because I liked the nickname, Little Rickey. But he still sounded sad. I needed to cheer him up.

"Hey, Mr. Gregor," I said. "Do you know what Willie Mays' nickname was?"

"Of course," he said.

"Then what was it?"

"The Say Hey Kid."

"Yep, yep," I said, grinning and swinging the plastic bag back and forth by my side.

"Told you I knew," he said, and winked at me. "Now I got one for you."

"'Kay, c'mon," I said, holding the bag still.

"What's Reggie Jackson's nickname?"

"Mr. October!" I said.

"Well, all right," he said, laughing, and put his hand over the fence so I could slap him five, and I did. Good. He wasn't sad anymore.

As we talked like good ol' buddies who knew our sport, I was thinking I was the only person he had a good talk with in years. Then he told me he had a baseball card collection of his own. With real autographs on three of them. From The Say Hey Kid, Joe DiMaggio, and Satchel Paige. *What?!* And a couple autographed balls too, one signed by Jackie Robinson himself. *Are you kidd—* "When can I see 'em?"

I said.

After clearing his throat a few times, he said I'd have to ask my parents to see if I could go over his house, since the items were put away. I told him my dad was working and my mom was sleeping, though I had a feeling he knew this already. He said I'd have to wait till my mom was awake. *Wait? Wait for what?* I just said okay and that I'd be right back.

I ran up the driveway, pretending like I was going to ask my mom. All I did was go inside the house and hide behind the side door, wait awhile, and run back out with the answer. "Yes. She said yes!"

I ran down the driveway and slipped but didn't fall. I still had the plastic grocery bag in my hand with trash in it. I hung it on the fence post and skipped toward the front gate of my new friend. But he was standing behind his gate with his head cocked to the side, looking at me like I'd done something wrong. "It's not good to tell a lie," he said.

I looked at the ground and sighed, thinking he must've seen the door move or something when I hid behind it. And now I wasn't going to see his collector's items because I couldn't keep still. *Dang it.*

"I'll let you slide this time," he said. "But listen,

since you didn't ask your mom, you can't tell her you came over here. You can't tell anybody, okay?"

I said okay and got happy again. He unlocked and removed the padlock before pulling the gate open. I walked in. I saw the rose bushes close up and got a good whiff. I turned around when I heard the gate close, saw him locking it back.

"Come on, son," he said, walking past me toward the steps. As I followed on the red cement path that he swept so often, I stopped. Something wasn't right.

I thought of what my Sunday school teacher, Mama Cece, said about the forbidden fruit in the Garden of Eden. "Forbidden means you are not to do it, don't go near it, stay away from it." And because my thoughts of going into Mr. Gregor's yard were always wrong, to me his yard was forbidden. But wasn't it different now that I wasn't sneaking to get a ball or to steal roses? Wasn't it different now because he invited me?

"Come on in," he said, holding the screen door open.

I looked at my house and was just about to tell him that's okay, I'll see the autographed cards and stuff another time. But after hearing him say, "Little Rickey, it's all right," and then me looking at his Pendleton . . . I went up the steps and walked into his house.

NINE

It was bright inside. All the lights were on. I almost asked him why he didn't just open the curtains and let the sun shine through, save some electricity. But I thought that would be rude.

It was just like old people's houses, with old-fashioned lamps and crystals hanging off the shade, plastic covering on the couch, black and white photos hanging around, and that funky smell of mothballs. (Back then I didn't know what that smell was. I just knew it was the smell of old people's houses.)

Above the couch in the center of the room hung a huge picture of a lady wearing a black hat. Her face was big and round and mean-looking, unlike Mr. Gregor's. Her black eyes stared right into mine, like she was saying, "What the hell you doing in my house?" I knew then the lady was his dead wife Advil.

The next room was the kitchen. Mr. Gregor told me to sit at the table so he could get what I came to see. But before I sat, I almost forgot what I came for. There was junk food all over the place. He had

Lay's Potato Chips, the plain and barbeque flavors on the table. All types of cookies from chocolate chip to Oreo. And I almost lost my mind when I saw two of my favorite types of cookies—Circus Animal and Iced Oatmeal Mother's Cookies. *Mr. Gregor is fresh.* And to top it off, behind a big bag of Doritos on the counter was a jar of my favorite type of candy ever invented by man: red licorice. It was heaven at Mr. Gregor's.

The only time I'd seen a big jar like that was on top of the counter at the liquor store around the corner. For a minute I wanted the snacks more than I wanted to see the baseball stuff. I called Mr. Gregor and asked if I could have some licorice and cookies.

"Did you eat breakfast?" he said.

"Yes," I lied.

He came into the kitchen and went straight to the licorice. None of the snacks, other than the chocolate chip cookies on the table, had been opened. I was going to ask why he had all these sweets, especially since he didn't have any friends. But he was over there grunting because he couldn't get the plastic seal off from around the top of the licorice jar with his fingers. Finally, he went in the drawer and got a Swiss Army knife. The seal came off. I rubbed my palms together under the table and thought of asking if I could come over his house whenever I wanted to. I was turning into my little brother.

He opened the jar and set it on the table in front of me, and said, "Have as many as you want, but don't eat too many." *Huh?* I just said okay and that I could open the bag of cookies myself. He nodded, said he'd be right back, and left. While he was gone, I tried to eat as much licorice as I could. *What a cool old man.*

There were three chairs at the table. I swung my legs back and forth while sitting in one of them, the other two were across from me against the wall, blocked by the table. The thought of Mr. Gregor being lonely crossed my mind. *I think I need to be his friend.*

At the end of the table was a small gray portable TV. Wait! Could this be the TV his wife died watching? I thought about what Aunt Ang' had said. I looked at the floor and imagined the mean-looking lady in the picture lying next to my feet, dead. But I shook it out of my mind. Aunt Ang' probably made that up.

The refrigerator was yellow, so was the counter, and so was the window curtain next to it. The same curtain we'd see him peeping from behind. It hung just above a garbage can with no lid. I grabbed a handful of Circus Animal Cookies and got up, pulled the curtain back with my free hand. Then I looked out at my yard as if I was Mr. Gregor.

I opened my hand to separate the white cookies from the pink ones, and accidentally dropped a white one in the garbage can. "Dang it," I said, watching it slide off a stack of folded brown paper bags from Emby. I saw something familiar in the corner where the cookie landed, and bent down to get a better look. Just as I thought: empty baseball card wrappers.

TEN

When I turned to walk back to the table, I saw a gun above the door in the hallway. The long kind made of wood and metal. Like the kind the police used to shoot at Rambo with. I didn't think it was real because it looked old and dusty and had scratches and scuff marks on it. Right next to it hung a plastic green shark. I wanted to touch the gun, but it was too high for me to reach.

The table had a lot of newspapers on it, with a fold down the middle from being delivered. Most were underneath the cookies and chips and stuff. Everything sat on the kitchen table and counter like he'd been grocery shopping just for snacks, or just for me. But I didn't think anything of it. And why should I? He had my favorites right there in front of me. I mean the licorice was enough by itself. Yes, they happened to be the same licorice I could be seen eating outside with my friends, the same ones I'd buy for three cents each at the liquor store around the corner. But he said I could have as many as I wanted. It gets no better than that! I had found a new friend, or, should I say, he found me.

My mouth was stuffed with licorice when I heard him call for me. "Son."

I answered the best I could. "Hmmm?"

"I need your help with something. Need you to give me a hand."

When I got up from the table to walk down the hallway, I saw a naked white woman on the wall calendar beside the refrigerator. I stared with my mouth open, my feet moving, but slowly, slowly, past her. I didn't notice until after he called for me again that I was drooling red saliva on my black sweatshirt.

"Where are you?" I said, brushing my arm against the spit on my chest.

"Come all the way back."

I passed by the closed door on my left with the gun above it and a barely open door to my right, where I saw a toilet. A narrow door was straight ahead at the end of the hall, and another closed door to the right of it. The one on the left was open a little. It was the room I found him in.

A closet with sliding doors was to my left, and a long dresser was right next to me to my right, pushed back against the wall. The dresser faced the foot of the bed. Mr. Gregor was straight ahead, reaching for something under the side of the bed. He got up when he heard me at the door, said one of his autographed balls had rolled under.

"Now I need you to crawl under there and get it for me, 'cause I'm too big to fit under a bed, you know," he said, laughing.

"Okay," I said.

He placed his hand on my shoulder and led me to the side of the bed. I got on my knees to take a look. He got on his knees too, and leaned, slightly, on me. I lifted the cover hanging off the bed to see better underneath. I saw a bunch of mess. I didn't see any ball.

When I turned around and asked where the ball rolled to, Mr. Gregor's face was right there, so close he could've kissed me. I jerked my head back. "Uh," he said, "it went somewhere behind the books under there, toward the head of the bed. Go 'head, take another look, huh."

I lay down to crawl under, and he put his hand on my lower back. He rubbed, right above my butt, as if he was guiding me to where the ball was. I slid quickly underneath, losing his hand. When I felt his hand again on my leg, I crawled farther and tried to play it off by saying, "I think I see it."

As I crawled on the hardwood floor past all the dust-covered papers, pennies and pens, pictures and shoes, and books but no ball, I wondered what I was doing in this stranger's house. I wanted to go home. I sneezed from all the dust and hurried from underneath the bed a little upset, a little nervous. I bumped my head hard on the way out. He helped me to my feet as if I couldn't get up by myself and talked in a really soft voice, like my dad does when he tries to make up with my mom.

"You okay?" he said, rubbing my head. "You didn't hurt yourself, did you?"

My lips trembled. My eyes watered. I couldn't answer.

I was afraid, and the back of my head was hurting. But I didn't cry. I walked away, telling him I didn't see the ball, that I'd check the other side of the bed. I was trying to get him to stop touching me. But when I got in the aisle between the foot of the bed and the dresser against the wall, I was in a worse position. He stood behind me, grabbed my arm and turned me around.

"It's okay," he said, soft and slow, "there's nothing to be afraid of. Here, let me clean you off." He picked the dust balls off of my sweatshirt near my chest.

"I can do it," I said, moving his hands away, but he brought them back. "I said I can do it."

"It's okay," he said. "Just let me clean you off . . . there's nothing to be afraid of, Little Rickey." He started unzipping my sweatshirt, and he squeezed my wrist real tight when I tried to stop him. The sweatshirt came off.

ELEVEN

I didn't know what to do. When he let my wrist go, I rubbed it against the side of my jeans 'cause it hurt. I felt the licorice sticking out that I had stuffed in my pocket. I pulled out two pieces, bit one, offered him the other. He didn't care. He just told me I could have as much candy and sweets as I wanted, anytime I wanted them.

"Well, look here," he said about my candy-stuffed pocket, "you got a whole bunch down here." He slid his hand down toward my pocket. I jumped back. Around the same time, I tasted dust in my mouth from the licorice I'd bitten on and started spitting.

Normally, whenever I spit I was just being cool or acting like a baseball player—like Boobee in his games before he threw a pitch. But spitting must have done something to me, because at that moment, I felt brave.

My dad always told my brother and me, "Never let anybody pick on you—no matter how big they are. Always stick up for yourself." NEVER LET ANY-BODY . . . NO MATTER HOW BIG . . . NEVER!

. . . ANYBODY! I kept hearing my dad's voice in my head. I wasn't scared to fight any kid around my neighborhood if he wanted a piece of me, but this was different. This was a grownup. And anyway, he didn't want to fight. He wanted something else.

What was I to do? In the streets, any man who liked another man the way men liked women was called a faggot. So I had to stick up for myself because this faggot was picking on me. He stood there, smiling the most two-faced smile I'd ever seen. But I didn't smile back. I was nervous, but not scared anymore.

From the corner of my eye I noticed the bedroom door was shut. He must've kicked it shut when I was under the bed. (Sly old bastard.) And I was just starting to think that Mr. Gregor was cool, and was going to teach him how to catch and bunt and throw a ball so he wouldn't have to drop it over the fence anymore. But now look: Mr. Gregor, a sixty-something-year-old grown man in his bedroom, with me, a seven-year-old boy.

He came closer, got on his knees, face to face with me. Whatever his next move was going to be, I had decided to make mine first. I tucked in my bottom lip, bit down, and with all my strength I gave my best kick. "Yah!" I had kicked him where it hurts all men, no matter how big or small, how young or old. He groaned and grabbed himself, dropped his head. Then I kicked him again real fast, same place. "Ooooo," he said. He leaned forward and reached out for me but went back immediately to holding his bruised "autographed balls."

Mr. Gregor rocked back and forth on his knees like he was going to fall over. So the next time he rocked forth, I popped him on the mouth with a palm strike. He made a funny noise and fell over. Another good move.

I put my hands down on the mattress and pushed off, swinging my legs and body over to the side. He moaned and groaned and pulled some of the blanket off the bed to put between his legs. I helped him by yanking it all off and throwing it over his head (a trick I always used on Kenny).

I noticed my sweatshirt lying under his back. I grabbed one of its sleeves and kept yanking it till I got it free. When I turned to leave, his hand came out from under the cover and pulled my ankle. I hopped on my other foot but lost my balance, fell. As he pulled my ankle, I kicked with the other foot. But he got a hold of my kicking foot too and took it under the cover. He had me.

"Where you going . . . huh?" he said, sounding angry and in pain.

"Let me go," I said. "I'ma tell my daddy." I sat up and pounded on his hands with my fists. "Let me go, you faggot!"

"I'll show you a faggot all right," he said.

Pounding his hands with my fists didn't work, so I squirmed till I ended up on the side of the bed where I had crawled under. I latched onto the bed's wooden frame, but he tugged my legs, and I lost my grip.

"Let. Me. Go."

I felt like my legs were being swallowed. When I was able to go under the bed some, I tried to find something that could hurt him, but the only thing near me was a book. A big hardback. He pulled me out from under the bed, and me and the book slid out.

I fought to turn over, to sit up. I held the book tight and lifted it above my head, then chopped down on his hands and head. "Aahhh!" he went, so I kept doing it till he let my legs go. The book had worked!

I dropped the hardback and scrambled to my

feet, headed for the door. He called me every name but Little Rickey as he struggled on the floor after me, his arm tearing pages from the book that fell open.

"Goddammit, look what you made me do!" he shouted. When I turned and looked down, I saw big letters on one of the ripped pages that read: The Holy Bible.

His head was near the door, so I swung that sucker open with all my might. Whack! The old man hollered. I had to step on his arm to squeeze through the door. He cussed. He threatened. I ran.

In passing the kitchen, I glanced out the window where I had pulled the curtain back and saw my mother in our yard. I ran to the window and banged. "Mama! Mama! I'm right here!"

With a terrified look on her face, Mama ran toward me. But what could she do? The window was barred.

"Go to the front—the front door, Mama," I said, pointing to the front of the house.

In the living room, I pushed the window curtain aside and saw my mama jump over the side fence and rush up the steps. I went to the door. Locked: one knob lock, two deadbolts, and one chain door lock. I unlocked the first two with no problem, stood on tip-toes to unlock the third, but I couldn't reach the chain lock. It was higher and thicker than any chain lock on any door I'd ever seen. I looked back when I heard the bedroom door opening and shutting.

"I got something for you," Mr. Gregor said. "Just wait. You just wait!"

I opened the front door as far as the chain lock allowed me, and yelled through the little crack of air, "Come on, Mama, he tryna come." But Mama couldn't get past the locked screen door, and my hand wouldn't fit all the way through the crack to unlock it.

"Hold on, baby, hold on," she said, banging and pushing on the screen.

"He's a fag, Mama! A faggot!"

"Okay, baby. Jus' hold on, 'kay? Mama's here—jus' hold on."

"I can't . . ." I kept yanking the door, "open it . . . Mama. I can't do it!"

"Okay, ba—" her voice broke. "Help me, Jesus."

It frightened me to see her frightened. I cried.

I had thought of grabbing the chair from the kitchen to try and reach the chain lock, but first I had to make sure Mr. Gregor wasn't coming. I glanced at the old woman on the picture. She looked even meaner. I turned back to Mama when I heard the screen crack and crack some more as she banged against it.

"Hold it, boy." It was Mr. Gregor coming down the hallway, bouncing from wall to wall, holding his privates with one hand, his bleeding head with the other.

"Here he come, Mama!"

"Damn right," Mr. Gregor said. "Here I come."

He was getting closer. He kept looking above the door, where the shark was, where the gun was. I watched, unsure of myself, as he brought down the gun.

"I got something for everybody," he said.

"Mama . . . I think he gotta gun."

"He what?! Oh, Lord," she said, and yanked the screen door open. "Stand back, baby."

I stepped aside, and through the door crack I saw her leg raise and stomp on that door, "Uh!" And I turned and saw Mr. Gregor leaning against the door with the shark above it, after picking up a black thing off the floor and putting it into the gun.

And Mama tried again, "Uh!" and she backed up and used her shoulder, "Mmm!" and she backed up and said, "Help me. Corey's in here!" in one breath to someone I couldn't see. And Mr. Gregor grunted something, and when I turned around the gun was by his eye. Pointed at me.

And Mama stomped again, "Uh!" and the door opened some, the screws in the wall were loose and sticking out—*Almost got it, Mama.* When she kicked again the door flew open. Someone behind Mama had just bust through Mr. Gregor's gate. I saw him just as Mama grabbed my hand. It was the Hulk.

TWELVE

"Come on," Mama said, grabbing my arm, and "Watch out, Gary, he gotta gun he gotta gun . . . molester!" she said to Mr. Brown, but too late, he was already in the house.

I ran into the rose bushes and got scratched by its thorns for looking back to see what was going to happen, like the lady in the Bible who turned to salt for looking back at what God was doing to Sodom and Gomorrah. I saw that the gun had somehow gotten on the floor and was kicked away by Mr. Brown, and saw Mr. Gregor fly backward after getting socked in the mouth.

Mrs. Brown came down the sidewalk in her nightgown, shouting, asking what happened and if we were okay. My mom mumbled something as we hurried past her to get to our yard. I glanced at Mr. Gregor's kitchen window from our yard. Didn't see anything, but I heard screaming I never knew a man could make.

When we got into the house, Mama grabbed the phone off the armrest, held me tight against her side as she dialed. "Yes, hello," she said into the phone. "My neighbor's gotta gun . . . and I think he kidnapped and—oh my God—he may have molested my son!"

"What?!" said Mrs. Brown, who must've heard from outside, the soles of her slippers made scratching noises up the steps. She was breathing as if she'd just finished running a marathon, with a look on her face like she'd been cheated out of first place. "I tell you what, Corrina," she said, her arms spread out against the doorframe. "You betta tell 'em hurry up. Gary gon kill that man. Girrrl, he's gon kill him!"

Almost immediately, we heard the sirens. Two cop cars pulled up in front of our house, two cops hopped out of each. Mrs. Brown ran toward them, lost one of her slippers but kept going, and pointed to Mr. Gregor's house while telling them to hurry.

It took all four policemen to get Mr. Brown out of the house. Mrs. Brown and my mom were outside, trying to get him to calm down by the soft tone of their voices, as the cops put him into the back of the police car.

I hurried and sat on the couch before my mom came back inside. She grabbed the phone and walked back and forth, mumbling, trying to figure out how to call my dad and explain things. She must've figured it out, because she dialed as she stood by me, put the phone to her ear, and brushed dust balls out of my hair while tapping her foot against the floor. Then she stopped tapping her foot, and she said to me, "Why do you have candy sticking out of your pocket?"

My mom and I were sitting on the couch in front of the living room window when we heard a car skid outside. We turned around at the same time.

"Corrina!" Mrs. Brown yelled from outside.

"Stay right here, baby," my mom said to me before she ran out of the house, leaving the door open.

My dad was already out of the car before my mom had gotten a foot out of the house. With my knees sunk into the couch pillows, I watched from behind the sheer curtain as he ran to each police car, yelling and cussing and asking, "Where is he?!"

My mom and Mrs. Brown tried to grab him, yell to him, make him believe that the ambulance followed by a police car had already taken Mr. Gregor away. After that, my dad came rushing toward the house, and I rushed to turn around and sit down before he came in.

My dad knelt down in front of me. Told me to look at him, but I couldn't. He grabbed my arms and stood me up. My mom came in and stood behind him, rubbed his back as he talked to me. "Are you okay? Huh? Did he touch you?" He lifted my chin up, but I kept my eyes on the floor. "What did he do? Corey, look at me. What did he do?!"

He started cursing the world, the neighbor, even himself, for not being there. Then he went quiet. He put my head against his chest. We stayed like that for awhile. I felt ashamed, not only of the mess I had caused, but because I was crying. And I never—well, I hardly ever—cried. Hardly ever.

A policeman brought my sweatshirt I'd left at Mr. Gregor's. "This belong to you?" he asked. I nodded. The cops then talked to my parents, then my parents talked to me and said the cops wanted to talk to me about what happened. So I sat in my living room, listening to a cop talk to me like a child, asking questions I wouldn't answer. Can you believe it, to get me to talk, the cop even offered me candy.

My mom stepped in. "It's okay, Corey. You can tell him."

So I ended up telling the cop the story, embarrassed my parents were hearing the story too. I talked slowly, my head down the whole time.

THIRTEEN

The policemen pulled my dad into the kitchen and spoke in low tones. But I still heard them, explaining how everything would be taken care of, and that because they had children and can understand and even see themselves reacting in the same way, they would release Mr. Brown. Until then, the Hulk was still in the police car, hopefully changing back into David Banner.

It's a good thing Kenny wasn't there the whole time. The babysitter, Ms. Rodriguez, had come from down the street to get him. He didn't understand what had happened, just knew something was wrong. When my mom was all hysterical on the phone with the cops, he ran and grabbed her leg, started hollering. Looking up at her face for an explanation, he kept pulling her leg, kept hollering till she gave him one.

She had to hug and kiss and promise him things till he hushed enough for Ms. Rodriguez to take him. So that's where he stayed till my mom, dad, and me came back from the hospital. I had to be examined: standard procedure.

The doctor noticed the dry saliva on my sweat-shirt and asked me how it got there. I told him what I told the cops. "Um. When I was chewing, this um, candy . . . I had, um, like, opened my mouth." I opened my mouth a little to show him. "And then like . . . some spit had um, accidentally came out."

The doctor just sat there looking at me. I think he knew I was leaving out something, but I wasn't going to tell him *what* or *who* made me drool. So I just kept swinging my legs back and forth off the side of the bed to get him to move on to the next question.

He did. He asked me to take my sweatshirt off. I did, and my mom told him the scratches on my arm got there from the rose bushes. He believed her, but then he asked me to take off the rest of my clothes. *For what, shooooot?* I sucked my teeth and asked why. He told me but it didn't matter. That doctor looked me all over and touched my body more than Mr. Gregor had. I hated it.

FOURTEEN

The sun was shining when we returned home in the afternoon. The word had gotten out. Uncles and aunts, girl and boy cousins, and friends of ours were already there. Mrs. Brown had stayed at our house, letting them inside till we got back.

The men were in the backyard with my dad, talking and playing music. And the women were in the living room, where I was, on the couch between Kenny, resting his arm on my leg, and my mom, who was rubbing my back. I never liked being babied. Any other time I would've said, "'Kay, Mom, thanks and stuff, but I'ma split and hang with the fellas." But I didn't. I stayed put. Safe. I needed her, and she came.

Tears fell from her eyes every few sentences as she talked about other things. She wiped them away like they were interrupting her conversation. My cousins and friends were on the porch at the screen door, pressing their faces against the screen. They gestured with their heads and hands for me to join them. I read their lips as they mouthed, "Come on. Come outside. What the heck are you doing?" Then Aunt Angie showed up, and started popping them upside the head. "Y'all need to move. I can't even see the color of the steps—go play somewhere."

Aunt Angie sat on the couch across from me, said she knew why the police came so fast. Said they were around the corner where a man had dragged his girlfriend outside by her hair. "The good thing is the girl had a weave, see, and this fool boyfriend of hers tryna to drag her, but she whatn't comin' . . . her hair was. Weave fallin' all down the stairs . . . and when he heard the sirens, the fool took off runnin' with tracks still in his hand." All the grownups laughed.

"The fuzz caught him on 104th and East 14th at the bus stop, tryna blend in with e'rybody else. He had sense enough to drop the tracks, but the damn fool had hair all over his white T-shirt." They laughed again, especially Mrs. Brown. My mom smiled. Aunt Ang' had changed the mood.

But she couldn't stop there, no no, not Aunt Ang'. "Come here, boy," she said to me from across the room. "Come out from under ya mama." I walked over, couldn't help smiling. "You all right?" she said. I nodded. "Good, 'cause Auntie didn't wanna hafta lift the mattress and get the fo-five. I woulda shot e'rybody, mm-hm, on accident. 'Cause Auntie don't know how to aim, she jus' know how to shoot."

She kissed the top of my head, then stood and told Mrs. Brown to run to Emby with her. She walked toward the front door, and my cousins and friends started ducking and scattering, laughing as they jumped off the porch. "Y'all better run, ya li'l punks," she said, stopping at the screen door. She took a cigarette from her purse, placed it between her lips and turned to me. "Rocky Road, right?" she said. I nodded.

FIFTEEN

The investigators had already left Mr. Gregor's house, and I had just sat on the porch with my cousins and friends, when Mighty Mike's Granada came flying around the corner. Two cars followed him, teenage boys packed in all three. "Uh-oh, here comes trouble," my aunt Jackie said under her breath as she stood behind the screen door, then yelled for Boobee's mom. "NeeNeeeeee."

The cars had stopped in the middle of the street. Boobee jumped out of the Granada, looking ready to fight somebody, Mighty Mike right after.

"Eh, Corey," Boobee said, walking fast into the yard. "Lemme holla at you." I got up and met him. He put his arm around my neck and walked me on the grass. "You ah-ight?" he said.

"Yee-ah."

"What happened, li'l cuz?"

"Wait, Boobee," said Aunt NeeNee busting out of the house, my cousins parting out of her way.

"Mama, I'm jus' tryna rap wit' my li'l cousin."

"No!—"

"I can't rap wit' my li'l cousin?"

"No!" she said again, walking toward him. "I won't allow you to get riled up and do something stupid."

"I ain't tryna hear that, Mama."

"Well, you need to—"

"It's too late for all that—you think somebody gon mess with Corey and I ain't gon do nothin'?"

"You don't need to do nothin'," my mom said, coming down the steps, Aunt Jackie behind her.

"Yeah," Aunt NeeNee said, "don't worry, Boobee. Mr. Brown hurt him pretty bad, it's okay now."

"Naw, Mama, it ain't okay. Now where he at, Highland?"

Aunt NeeNee sighed, didn't answer his question about Mr. Gregor being at the county hospital. She was breathing hard, her chest going up and down.

"I *knew* potna whatn't cool," Boobee said, "'member I told you, li'l cuz?"

"Mm-hmm," I said.

"You need to calm down, baby," his mother said.

Boobee walked back and forth, cussing about not needing to calm down. A car came down the street and couldn't get by, started honking. Two of Boobee's friends, Tidy Bo and DJ, jumped out of the car and cussed the man out, told him to turn around and go the other way. The man did, no problem.

"Look," Aunt NeeNee said, holding her son by his arms, "we're about to cook some fish—um, y'all park the cars and come on in."

Tidy Bo asked Boobee what he wanted to do, looking ready to do whatever he said.

"Nothin'," my mom said to Tidy Bo. "I already told you y'all don't need to do nothin'."

"Somebody get Keith," Aunt NeeNee said. "Corrina, go get my brother, please."

"Keith." My mom shouted my dad's name as she walked backward toward the backyard, keeping an eye on the boys. "Keeeeith."

"Come on, blood, we out," Boobee said to Mighty Mike before they jogged to the car and jumped in; Tidy Bo and DJ too.

"Keeeeeith."

"Li'l cuz," Boobee said, and motioned his head for me to come. I ran to the car. "I told you what'll happen if potna stepped out of line, right?"

"David, come here," my dad said, calling Boobee by his real name as he came quickly around the corner with the other men. Boobee looked at him, then back at me.

"Won't be firecrackers, li'l cuz. Won't—"

"David!"

"—be firecrackers. Mighty." And Mighty Mike burned rubber while Aunt NeeNee and the grownups called for Boobee to come back. In seconds, all three cars were down the street.

"Umph, umph, umph," Uncle Vick said. "That ain't never a good sign. Never a good—"

"Victor!" my dad cut him off.

Like all of us, Aunt NeeNee kept her eyes focused down the street. A few seconds later she was shaking her head and covering her mouth with her hand, sniffling. My mom saw and put her arm around her. They walked slowly toward the house. Uncle Vick looked at the ground and began shaking his head too, walking toward the backyard, mouthing to himself and no one else, "Never a good sign . . ."

SIXTEEN

We had fish, fries and red Kool-Aid for dinner. Some of my boy cousins were fighting over who would sit next to me. It almost became a big party for a hero—ME? They wanted the man of the hour to give them the scoop. I was going to keep quiet because I felt funny about what a man tried to do to me. But because they treated me like a star, I had to give them something. They huddled up as I whispered.

I told them he didn't touch me at all, but tried to. (I mixed truth with lies.) My nine-year-old cousin Jario, a mama's boy, corrected me when I said Mr. Gregor was a faggot. "Don't you mean molester?" he said. Everybody sucked their teeth and told him to shut up and go somewhere. I knew that was the proper word to use, my mom and the cops had said it earlier. But Jario was being smart.

So my six-year-old cousin Donald, a little comedian, and the only one of us with a Jheri curl, stood up in his chair and pointed across the table at Jario. "*You* a faggot!" he said, and we all busted up laughing.

And Donald was smiling and taking it all in, when my mom came storming into the kitchen, asking who said it. Jario told her, and she told Donald that unless he was getting ready to preach a sermon, he better sit his narrow behin' down in his chair. All of us, she said, better keep that bad word out our mouths. She even glanced at me because she had heard me yell the word earlier.

Then she said to Donald: "And you, little boy, you say it again and I'ma set every last one of them curls on fire." Everyone except Donald and me snickered. "You hear me?"

"Yes, Aunt Rina."

"I don't know what a little boy doing with a perm anyway," she said on her way out.

After seeing how irritated we got at him for getting Donald in trouble, Jario took his plate in the living room and sat with his mommy. Then I had an idea. "Eh, check it out," I said, whispering again. "Why don't y'all see if y'all could spend the night?" I'd continue the story then, I told them. They loved the idea.

When I walked out of the kitchen, Aunt Angie must have just walked in. I heard her ask who wanted ice cream, and of course everybody said, "Meeee."

She asked where I was, and they told her I went to the bathroom 'cause that's where I said I was going. Though I did have to pee, I wanted to know what Mr. Brown did to make Mr. Gregor scream.

So I snuck out the side door into the dark and tiptoed along the side of the house. When I got near the back, I got on my knees and peeked around the corner. The men were sitting on old raggedy chairs in the middle of the backyard, where the light hanging off the house could hit them. I saw the back of Uncle Vick, wearing that same dirty green and yellow A's hat that he always wore backward. I noticed he rocked back and forth in his seat as Mr. Brown talked.

". . . knocked him down the hall, and that's when I saw Corey's sweatshirt on the floor. And maaan, seeing that was like throwin' gasoline on a fire."

Uncle Vick jumped up holding a forty-ounce bottle of beer in one hand, pointing his finger up in the air with other. "Speakin' of fire," he said, "that ol' fool shoulda been burned alive."

"I hear you, Vick, I hear you," Mr. Brown said. "But I think he got what he deserved."

"Yeah, I guess," Uncle Vick said and sat back down.

"Y'all know they used M1 carbines in WWII and Korea, right?" Mr. Brown said. "Yes, sir. Fifteen rounds a clip."

"Damn," Uncle James said, "imagine if it was loaded."

"It *was* loaded."

"Whaaaat?"

"Cocked and ready," Mr. Brown said. "Cops checked it out—tell 'em, Keith."

"Yep."

"And he must've cocked it and dropped it, 'cause he didn't have the gun in his hand when I saw him. Don't ask me why, don't ask me how, all I know is if he had pulled that trigger . . . your brother Keith here woulda went after him and everybody with the same last name."

That's when Uncle Vick jumped up again, this time slamming his bottle of beer on the ground—shattering the glass, fizzling the beer. He started cussing, and Uncle James too, the worst I've ever heard them, explaining how they wanted to hurt Mr. Gregor in the most painful of ways. And not just Mr. Gregor, but any molesters like him.

My dad sat on the seat of the bench press with

his arms folded and said nothing. But when Uncle Vick was the only one still cussing and fussing, my dad waited till he sipped his new bottle of beer before he talked.

"So," my dad said to Mr. Brown sitting beside him, "what woke you and Sharon up anyway? Y'all usually sleep in till what, 'bout ten-thirty, eleven?"

"Yeah, that's about right," Mr. Brown said, smiling a little. "But believe it or not, Junior woke me up. He was in the living room, laughin' at cartoons—and I mean laughin' hard, Jack, like we do at Richard Pryor, ya dig. And you know me, I can sleep through anything."

"I know," my dad said.

"But once I got up, I couldn't go back. So I said I may as well go in the garage and mess around on the six-fo. It's been over a year since I worked on it. So I took a shower, threw on some clothes, shook the bed—told Sharon get her butt up—then I went and fixed us some coffee. Sharon came in to cook breakfast, told her call me when it's done, and that's when I took my coffee and stepped outside."

It got quiet. My dad unfolded his arms, rubbed his chin, looked at the sky. "Isn't that something," he said. Then he turned to Mr. Brown. "Gary, I'm just glad you were there, man."

"Aw, man, you know."

"And I'm glad Gary Jr. woke you up just by laughing. I'm glad my wife was there too. I haven't asked her yet, but I got an idea what made her go outside. Seems like each one of y'all had a role to play. Like there was a man behind the curtain cueing y'all when to go on stage. Sometimes the man doing the cueing goes on stage himself. But only those who know him know that. The rest find out at the end."

"Hmm," Mr. Brown said. Then leaned back in his chair and stared at the ground. All the men seemed to be doing the same. It got quiet again. But then . . .

"No offense, Gary," Uncle Vick said, "but if it was my turn to go on stage, I woulda killed that sucka, shoot." (Only he didn't say "shoot.") "I woulda shot him with all fifteen of them rounds—every last one of 'em. Then looked for anotha clip to reload."

Mr. Brown looked at my dad. My dad looked back at him and shrugged.

"I gotcha, Vick, I gotcha," Mr. Brown said. "Well, from what I hear, nobody'll be hearing from ol' Gregor again. Not even Mr. Gregor."

"You say that like the fool's dead or in a coma or somethin'," Uncle James said, joking. Then he got serious. "Wait. You didn't kill him, did you? He ain't dead, is he?"

Everyone, including me, was waiting for Mr. Brown to answer, and he was fixing his lips to say something when some dummy opened the side door. "Coreeeey. Coreeeey," my brother called, and everyone looked my way. "There you go. Ant Angie lookin' fo you." I ducked my head back and tiptoed away. "We got Rocky Ro i-scream," he said.

It was too late to shssh him. I bit down on my lip and gave him "the look" as I walked toward him. I lifted my arm across my shoulder, ready to backhand him. He flinched when I got close to him and laughed hesitantly, hoping that I was playing. I nudged him into the house and followed behind, sucking my teeth, wondering if Mr. Gregor was dead.

SEVENTEEN

My cousins waited in my room after my dad called me into his bedroom. We were going to talk man-to-man. I sat on the edge of his bed beside him, staring at my feet.

"How you doing?" he said.

"Fine."

"Then look me in the eye," he said, and I did.

He faced forward and placed his elbows on his knees, his hands folded and pressed against his mouth. Quiet. While he thought about whatever he was thinking about, I couldn't stop wondering what happened to Mr. Gregor. I wanted to know hecka bad, but it was best I didn't ask—at least not now—because I was supposed to be in some kind of trouble here. I had to be patient and hear what the consequences of my stupid actions were going to be. And the consequences were coming, because my dad dropped his hands and leaned back, cleared his throat, quiet no more.

"I love you. And I care too much about what happens to you. Same goes for your brother. Same goes for your mother. It's important that you do what we tell you. What we say is going to help you," he said, and leaned in closer, "maybe even save your life.

"Nothing that man could've named is worth your life. No baseball memorabilia, no licorice, no cookies, no money—is worth your life. I don't care if he promised to take you to Malibu and Great America in the same day. They ain't worth it. I don't care if he promised you season tickets to the A's and the Giants games. I don't care if he's an uncle to Rickey Henderson, a cousin to Jackie Robinson, and a stepbrother to Ted 'The Thumper' Williams—nothing he could've named is worth your life."

A tear slid down my face. I felt him watching. As brave as I could, I looked back at him and saw the tears building in his. *Daddy, are you going to cry too?!*

"I'm sorry, Daddy."

He took a deep breath, put his arm around my shoulder and pulled me closer to him. Then he tilted his head back and looked at the ceiling, and grinned. "This my little man right here," he said, and put me in a headlock. I laughed. I was forgiven.

"Go on," he said. "Be with your cousins."

But I had to ask him—believing that I could get

a yes with all these emotions and stuff—if my cousins and I could stay up late.

"Yeah," he said, "I let you stay up late *every* Saturday. Who you think turns the TV off?" *Huh?* I was "moded." In other words, I felt stupid.

"But if your mama finds out, I'm not in it—you hear me?"

"Okay."

"And if you can't get up for church without turning into Oscar the Grouch, you can forget about staying up. I'll start sending you to bed at five in the evening."

"Five o'clock?"

"Four-thirty, if you want."

"Okay, okay," I said grinning. "I'll stop being like that."

"All right, go 'head. We finish talking."

I guess there was no reason to punish me because I had punished myself. For one, the trouble I got into was so bad it scared the mess out of me, had me crying—and people saw me crying too! Dang it! And two, a man wearing a white coat who calls himself a doctor made me strip so he could check my private parts. That was punishment enough.

EIGHTEEN

My cousins ended up sleeping over, so I kept my promise. I showed them how I kicked and punched the neighbor till I broke his jaw and cracked his ribs, then broke the glass bottle over his head, and cut him across the neck with the leftover part. I told them I kept flicking the piece of glass in his face, taunting him, asking him if he wanted more. (Okay, so I exaggerated, but I was only a kid.) Aunt Ang' had taught me well.

You should've seen their faces—I had 'em going. "Oooh, for real? Then what? Did you do him like this, cousin—look. Look, cousin. Did you do him like this—Hi-yah! Like this, huh?—Waaah!" They started punching and kicking and karate-chopping each other. Donald was in the corner of the room practicing the drop kick I'd showed them. His curls bounced every time he landed. He got so excited the f-word slipped out.

"Oooooh!" Jario said, "Aunt Rina said don't say that."

Donald turned around. "Shut up, punk," he

said, and punched our smart-aleck mama's boy cousin in the chest twice—"Mm! Mm!"

And Jario, being dramatic as always, stood with his mouth wide open and his eyes shut tight. He cried like a baby who'd lost his mom in the mall. No more play-fighting.

Only my eleven-year-old cousin JJ knew better than to believe the version I gave the youngsters. He sat on the top bunk with his back against the wall and hands behind his head, a smirk on his face. The whole time I tried not to look at him because we both knew I was putting on a show. Later I told him what really happened, and he was all cool about it like he already knew.

Kenny was quiet the whole night, sitting Indian-style on my bed throughout the performance. Before I knew it, he was lying on top of my covers. When I looked again he was sleeping under them. I guess the little fella loved his big brah. What can I say, I loved the kid too.

One by one, cousin by cousin, they fell asleep watching TV. Dubbed-in-English voices mixed in with the different levels of snoring. I got up to turn the TV off but changed my mind: I needed the company. I stood for a minute watching the different colors flash against the sleeping faces in the room. Blue, green, red.

I got into bed and watched TV awhile; but couldn't get into it so I turned toward the wall; but couldn't sleep, so I turned on my back. I stared at the long-bearded man I'd drawn in pencil on the cardboard, between the wooden slabs that kept the top bunk in place. He was a master: had a lot of wisdom, knew a lot of moves. Nobody could beat him.

Next to him I'd written the title of my favorite TV program, the one now playing, the one that had me sneaking for nothing to watch it. It reminded me, *I kicked a grown man!* I wondered why I didn't use the cooler moves I'd learned, like the snake and crane. *Man, that would've been fresh.* And I wondered if I moved as fast as The Centipede in the movie *The Five Venoms*. With these thoughts, there came a low tapping at the window. Even with the reflection of the TV on the windowpane, the bars on the window, and the black beanie on his head, I knew it was Boobee. I smiled, lifted the window.

"Sup, li'l cuz?"

"Sup, Boobee?"

He glanced over the room. "They sleep?"

"Yep."

"You the only soldier. Look, even JJ couldn't hang." He looked over at the TV and started grinning. "I see you watchin' eem, huh?"

"Yep."

"Keep learnin' them moves, li'l cuz."

"I am."

He reached into his pocket. "Here you go," he said, handing me an Oakland A's headband through the iron bars.

"Ah, fresh!" I said in a loud whisper.

"I keep my promises. And I'ma see if my homegirl can stitch number thirty-five on there for you later on—whatchu think?"

"That'll be fresh, thanks."

"You welcome. Now gimme five on the blackhand side," he said, even though both sides of his hands were black because of the burners he had on, the black leather gloves with holes at the knuckles.

I heard somebody moving outside, crunching on the leaves I didn't get a chance to rake that morning. Boobee looked where the noise came from and backed up a little, put his finger up to let whoever it was know he was coming. I noticed his black jogging suit.

"I'ma split, li'l cuz," he said. "Oh, and we found out ol' potna was gone bye bye before we could get to eem."

"Whaaaat?"

"Mr. Brown ain't no joke."

"For real?"

"For real, li'l cuz. Ding dong! The witch is dead. So me and my homies gon show you how we celebrate." Boobee slowly pulled his beanie down over his face, turning it into a ski mask. "And shut the window, li'l cuz. The parade's about to start." He put his finger to where the hole was for his lips, as if to shssh me, then threw the hood over his head and skipped away.

I was left facing the Browns' house, my heart beating fast. I knew what was about to happen. I pulled the window down but left a crack. I got up to turn the volume down on the TV and hurried back to the window. Before I could count to twenty, the parade had begun.

POPOPOPOPOPOPOPOPOPOP—and at the same time—BOOM! BOOM! BOOM! BOOM! Some of my cousins jumped out of their sleep, asking, "What was that?" Donald crawled up next to me, wearing my mom's shower cap, and put his ear to the crack also.

"Ooh! Somebody shootin', huh, Corey?"

"Well, it ain't no firecrackers, li'l cuz . . . ain't no firecrackers."

We heard laughing and cussing before the car doors slammed shut. Then the cars peeled off. The parade had ended.

My dad's feet thumped against the floor in his room before he came to check on us. While Donald and I played sleep, he told those who woke up it was okay to lie back down before he turned our light back off. Then he did a forward march to the front of the house. I wanted to go see, but my stupid door squeaked whenever it opened, and I'd already been in enough trouble for the day. After a few minutes we heard the front door shut, and my dad went grumbling back to his room. I got up to eavesdrop, put my ear to the wall. Donald did too, the shower cap made crinkling noises when he did. He stared at the A's headband on my head.

"Where'd you get that?"

"Shsssh," I said.

My mom asked my dad what just happened, and he said Mr. Gregor's house had been shot up. He could tell by the streetlights. He basically said there were enough holes in the house to play connect the dots and have a strange animal when you finished. Chunks of wood were blown off the house, and that stupid screen door, the front door and living room window, even the kitchen window on the side, were destroyed. You could see inside the house from outside. The curtain had fallen.

The rose bushes had their last day to be beautiful, their petals were scattered like red and white ashes along the red path. Like ashes. Along the red path. The sun would soon rise, but the day would never be over.

NINTEEN

It took a few days before my mom told me something about that day. Something I didn't know. I had wondered what she was doing outside the morning I saw her through Mr. Gregor's kitchen window. She never came outside while I did chores. She stayed in her room, even when I was done. That's why I thought I could fool Mr. Gregor and get away with it. She told me she was led to come and look for me.

"What do you mean 'led,' Mama?"

"I mean I was told to go and look for you."

"Somebody *told* you to look for me? Who?"

She put her arm around me and let it rest across my chest. "The Holy Spirit," she said.

The Holy Spirit? Come on now, Mama, tell me you wanted to get up early and get some fresh air, or tell me you wanted to see who this great landscaper of a son was that always made the yard look extra good. (That's right, extra). So I asked, "You mean while you were sleeping, the Lord woke you up and told you to go outside and look for me?"

"Sleeping?" she said. "Who said I was sleeping? I get up at six every morning to study The Word and pray. For two, sometimes three hours. I just happened to be praying for *you* when the Lord told me to go outside and check on you. So that's what I did. And as soon as I got outside in the yard," she snapped her fingers, "there you were, banging on the window. So no, Mama ain't sleeping, baby. And God ain't either."

It's not that I didn't believe she got up every morning to pray and stuff, 'cause Mama ain't a liar, but I had to ask my dad so he could help me understand better, or maybe believe better. I made sure my mom wasn't around. He told me the alarm clock I hear beeping through the wall wasn't just for him, but for her too. He got ready for work, she got ready for prayer.

My dad hardly ever went to church. It'd have to be Easter or Father's Day or something special like that for him to go. But after my mom told him what she told me, he went more often. In fact, he went the next day. My mom said that was one prayer she always prayed: that her husband would go to church regularly.

The incident brought my family closer to God,

and me closer to my mom. I was so grateful to see her through that window, running for me, and hopping that fence like a pit bull was behind her. And she did it with such ease, like she'd been practicing when nobody else was around. No stumbling, no tripping over the top—nothing. An undercover stunt woman. I brought this up, and she cracked up laughing. Other than being athletic in school, she said she didn't know how she did it, but that she didn't have a choice, she had to.

I thank God for finding a brave and godly woman, then choosing her to be my mother; and for a father, whose manliness came out of him and into me, and out of me when it was needed. My dad was cool, so cool he allowed me to stay up late on Saturdays to watch my favorite TV program, the one Boobee put me up on: Kung-Fu Theatre. Because, see, that is where I learned my moves.

Acknowledgments

Thanks to my mother, who has supported and loved me immensely, and told me since I was a child that I was talented. I grew up to believe her. To my siblings, for having faith in your brother and spreading the word. To my bumbling bee, Nai, whom I love and am proud of just because you're you; thank you for telling your teacher and classmates about your daddy and helping to arrange a class reading. I loved how, after hearing me read for nearly thirty minutes, they got attitudes and sucked their teeth when your teacher had to cut the reading short because it was lunchtime.

Anne Fox, my copyeditor, for wanting to help me because you saw something in my writings worth your attention, or simply, because you wanted to help *me*. I am grateful. And thanks for introducing me to the following two people I shall also thank: Mark Greenside, for your insight and knowledge about writing. I promise I learn something new every time you have the floor. And Charlotte Cook, for giving me writing game.

Thanks to Sgt. Petty, James "Sweet Lew," Rodshetta Smith, Joe Fowler, "Uncle" Curtis V., and my granddaddy "Dada," who were reliable sources. To my mama and her li'l sis Cheryl Jean, for letting me use their Internet for research. To Brenda Cheatham, for being you. To Tracy—"The Deveroux," for reading my stuff and getting excited that everyone who wanted to could soon read it too. Jackie Graves, for listening and helping me get back to writing after my mom went home to Jesus. To every writer who's given me feedback, especially my cousin Meshia—"The Jones Street Girl," Tanisha, and Gene Durnell, who all read the first draft.

A special thanks to my cousin Trestin George, for supporting me in every way, every time. Brian Mollath, for believing every acting performance of mine was worth checking out, every writing was worth reading, and for telling me to stop sitting on the couch and watching TV or sleeping or just being plain lazy, or whatever it was that was holding me back. Erin Breckenridge, for putting miles on your vehicle just to come see what I was going to do next, when nobody else (other than my mama) would even start their engine.

A.R. Smith, for getting excited that I had something worth getting excited for. Alena Jacks-Young, for answering the phone to hear new ideas I came up with, and for making me feel special by loving everything I write. Sarah Breed, my homegirl, for helping me and bragging about me and having my back. Mary Hurley, for being genuinely kind and taking the time to ask me where I was going, then helping me to see what I needed to get there. Ann Gallagher, my friend who loves to laugh, thank you for reading my stuff in one sitting, and believing in me and telling others why you do. Celestine Watkins and Pat Franklin, those lovely ladies who noticed me and pointed me out to other people, because they believed in me. They help me because they love me. (And I love y'all suga's too.) And right-on to Andre Wallace and J-Red, who were there for me before and after my mother died.

And lastly, thank you to my dear Layla Manna Embaye, who was chillin' with me when the concept of this story flowed out of me in the form of a freestyle poem; and for listening and enjoying my writings and telling me "I can't wait!" Well, the wait is over. I hope you enjoyed what it's turned out to be.

A shout-out to all those from West to
East Oakland that I grew up with in the 1980s.
Those were the days.